The Headless White Horse

A collection of stories by

Roger Colby

This is a work of fiction. Names, characters, places and incidents either are products of the author's imagination or are used fictitiously. Any resemblance to actual events or locales or persons, living or dead, is entirely coincidental.

The opinions in this manuscript are solely the opinions of the author and do not represent the opinions or thoughts of the publisher. The author has represented and warranted full ownership, and or legal right to publish all the material in this book.

Cover art by Jack Johnson

Twitter: Jack Johnson

ISBN: 0-9896841-5-6
ISBN-13: 978-0-9896841-5-6

Foreward

All of us have monsters that plague us. Mostly they are imagined. However, sometimes there are monsters who are real. All you have to do is turn on the news to find a few of them lurking around. Today's monsters are not really in movies or in our closet, but are leaders of countries where they are worshipped as gods or are elected by a misinformed populace.

The monsters found in this book will never visit you. They will never take away your health care or put you in prison for your beliefs. They are simple diversions, something to pass the time and get your mind off of the real monsters you face every day. It is my hope that you enjoy these little diversionary monsters and that after reading about some of them you won't be able to sleep.

Mostly I hope they make you talk about them around the water cooler. Hopefully they are memorable enough to do that at least.

Roger Colby

TABLE OF CONTENTS

To my Dad, who always told the best stories.

RUST

Roy thought that six days in a space suit was intolerable even for a convicted felon and so reluctantly decided that he would voice his concern to Managatron about it. He had suffered through long days of mining before, but never like this week. The chalky red rock of Mars chipped and scattered about him as he dug one of the deeper mines of his five year sentence.

Go mine Mars. Shorten your sentence.

In protest, he switched off the borer beam and set the clunky device on the rust red dirt. He thought about the unofficial prisoner motto, "greed must go on", the disgruntled mantra of all Mars miners, sentenced to the long hours of labor because of some crime or another, from petty theft to murder. Millions of them, digging like fire ants beneath the surface of this dead world with ice blue borer beams in hand, hoping to one day mine enough ore to satisfy their robot foremen, to satisfy a sentence. As he climbed aboard the mine elevator, his knees creaking painfully, he flipped a few switches, ignoring the auditory warning that his shift had not yet ended and that he would face another week of diminished food rations if he proceeded, and thought about Guari Hussar and whether or not she would ever remember him or even care that he ended up here, that she might forgive him.

She had such soft hair.

Even though the elevator's speed hurt his gut it took him ages to reach the surface. When the doors slid open he lumbered silently across the burnt orange landscape, his thick soles kicking rubble here and there, passing near the junky evacuation rocket that sat unattended and forgotten save the sentry guns that sprang to life at his approach and then powered down as he stalked away. Nearby stood Managatron 72343-4, Roy's warden, who turned methodically toward him, its yellow paint chipped and faded, rusty metal beneath, its somewhat humanoid appearance angular and slightly taller than Roy.

Intimidatingly taller.

"State the purpose for abandoning your shift, prisoner two, two, seven, three dash nine," came the deep voice that was lower than any human voice could manage, with a vibrato that buzzed Roy's helmet speakers.

"Request immediate break," said Roy evenly. "Prisoner two, two, seven, three dash nine is exhausted. I need a break."

"Designated meal break is not scheduled at this time. Please return to work immediately or face solitary confinement for the remainder of your shift plus nutrient feed via injection."

He had done that once. Unyielding metal arms locked him in a box where a micro-filament needle jabbed a vein once a day and made sure he kept up his strength. He decided to press it anyway.

"Request immediate break, seven, two, three, four, three dash four," he pleaded, tears beginning to well. "… Please."

It shifted on its metal legs and Roy saw a tiny spray of hydraulic fluid escape its left knee joint to glide out a few feet above the surface, little spinning globs of red on a burnt orange background that eventually settled to the dirt.

"Waste recycling unit on mining suit of worker two, two, seven three dash nine operating within parameters," it said, as if that were meant to help his situation. The suit recycled his urine and feces but he never got used to the taste of the drinking water or the idea of what it used to be. This statement was simply the routine of the company, the routine of the five or so automated statements that Managatron was programmed to say, and Roy had heard them all countless times. It followed up this statement with another, and Roy mouthed the words.

"Report immediately to your post, prisoner two, two, seven three dash nine," it droned. "Shift change in seven Martian hours. That is all."

Managatron turned and strode away, its knee spewing tiny red droplets, and Roy hung his head, his arms relaxing at his side. He could not remove his helmet, could not enter the air lock of mining base 224238-8 and fall into the shower stall, could not cram himself painfully into his efficient sleeping alcove, could not dream of Guari Hussar.

He turned, passed slowly by the forgotten escape rocket, paused briefly to consider facing the sentry guns to climb aboard, and then passed on by to enter the elevator and delve the twelve or so kilometers where he finally shuffled over to his borer beam. He winced as he hoisted it to his hip and began the slow process of chipping away at the company's precious ore, their greed having exhausted all resources on Earth.

The beam carved chunks of red rock, huge blocks crumbling down to the floor of the mine silhouetted by the ambient banks of LED lights, their soft glow making strange and horrible shadows on the walls, and then he broke through to a void, a cloud of compressed gas erupting into the room. He absent-mindedly ran the beam for a bit before shutting it down again, and dropping it to the powdery red dirt he crunched a few steps forward to peer into the inky blackness of the hole.

Reaching up to his helmet, he switched on his lamps and found a rust stained corridor, and even though he had not realized the significance of his find, the old stories of some lost Martian civilization buzzing in his brain, he stepped in through the hole delicately, his knees creaking, and put his hand on the sand paper walls.

"Recorder on," he stammered. "Found a shaft that doesn't appear to be natural. Investigating further."

"Prisoner two, two, seven, three dash nine, you have shut down your borer beam. Please continue wor—."

But the throaty voice of Managetron coughed and died in a sea of static as he moved further down the hallway within the void. Even though he could not hear his own footfalls, he felt a vibration beneath his soles, an energy, and the hallway stretched on into the darkness, his helmet lamps illuminating rusted walls, the outward edges slightly curved with no right angles. It felt like a rusty tube, like looking at the inside of a straw found in the garbage. He moved forward, noticing a soft red glow ahead of him, his arms outstretched to touch the walls with his heavy gloves, the rust flaking off and drifting to the floor in a fine dust.

He moved on, ignoring his stomach's message to his brain that he needed to eat, and he soon emerged in a titanic chamber the size of which caused his mind to nearly fail him. He stood at the edge of a dimly lit spherical room with long, rusted metal shafts that protruded from the walls toward the center in uneven patterns and in different lengths, the shortest of them to Roy seeming to be the length of that tower in Dubai before it fell in the war.

He walked for what seemed an hour toward the center, his helmet beams bouncing off of rusting metal surfaces, until he finally reached what could only be called a console, a raised dais with a podium shaped object, made of the same rusting metal, with what looked like a massive lever that protruded from the center. A groove the same size as the lever bifurcated the podium. He was not an archaeologist, but he thought that all of this must be extremely old, the builders long since abandoning their handiwork.

His dust covered, gloved hands reached out to touch the ancient console and he felt a vibration in his fingertips before they ever brushed the metal, an electricity thrumming beneath it, a power of age old technology. His hands moved to the lever, at least that is what he thought it was, a rusted metal shaft that rose from a groove in the top panel, a spherical knob at the end, the knob made from some black material that phosphoresced when his helmet lamps washed across it.

He pulled.

Nothing. It would not budge.

He removed a tool from his belt, a heavy metal hammer used for testing the density of ore, and he banged on it, the sound of which could not be heard in this place without air, but he could feel it through his glove, and he could feel something give as a paper thin sliver of rust fell from the lever.

He tried again, this time feeling it break loose and

pull toward him as if it willed itself to follow the movement
of his hands, and soon it was pulled completely toward him
and a yellow light began to glow beneath the rusted face of
the console, breaking out of the corrosion like the sun behind
storm clouds. He touched the light and another, a green
light, flashed beneath the yellow one and he moved his hand
there, and the massive cathedral of a room suddenly became
awash with an eerie blue light.

He bent backward at the waist and peering above
him saw a massive ball of bluish electric light pulsating and
growing larger, ominously causing his helmet speakers to
crackle to life with a feedback that made his teeth grind. His
hands rose instinctively to the sides of his helmet as if to
block out the sound, but it was of no use, the deafening
noise rattling his ear drums, the pain shooting through his
brain like a superheated ice pick.

He ran, turning back to where he had entered, his
feet falling soundlessly on the floor of the massive room, the
only thing audible to him the sound of the horrible feedback
and the rising tempo of his own breathing. He grunted,
nearly swooning, and found the entrance to the room
eventually, his head lamps bouncing around the severely
rusted walls, the rust falling in sheets from the ceiling, and
when he finally made it to the elevator, there was a
thrumming vibration in the ground that grew in intensity,
the dirt beneath his feet vibrating and rocking, his stomach
churning with absolute fear.

The elevator could not move fast enough, and
when it neared the surface it abruptly halted, something
above falling to smack the top of it, a rock perhaps, and he
climbed, his breath rasping, his knees arguing with him, up

the escape ladder to the surface only to find the outside world in chaos, the ground shaking with a magnitude beyond the human mind to grasp. His robot warden, pinned beneath a fallen chunk of rock, one broken metal arm waving at him as he staggered, the feedback subsiding, toward the escape rocket.

The sentry guns sprang to life, not giving any warning before firing their superheated beams at his arm first as a warning, but it was too late, and he glimpsed from the far right range of his visor a mist of escaping air and crimson. He fought through it, and a rock from a nearby cliff crashed down on one of the guns, the other firing again, this time burning a more mortal wound through his abdomen, but he fought through it.

He found the hatch, popping the safety loose with a trembling gloved hand, the ground shaking beneath him, the soundless horror of it all beyond his understanding, and as he climbed within the capsule and closed the door, the rocket lifting far above the crumbling surface of Mars. He felt the air normalize around him enough to remove his helmet, his wound feeling as if someone had taken a blow torch to his liver and then left a hot coal there.

He rose higher and higher, and he stared out of the single porthole, sweat pouring across his eyes, and saw the rust red planet of Mars breaking up, large chunks of the crust falling away, smashing into the orbiting processing stations and killing thousands, their hulls imploding and scattering like glitter on the black velvety backdrop of space.

But then he screamed, and could not stop screaming even though it hurt him so badly to do so, his precious blood bubbling from his stomach in small globules that floated in the zero gravity.

Inside the planet Mars, now revealed after eons of time, a massive machine, its insectoid legs extending outward, a city sized bolt of blue lightening flashing between metallic, rusted antennae, turned slowly, its crab-like metal carapace releasing millennia of space dust and red rock that had formed a planet around it, and as Roy slipped in and out of the blackness of oblivion, he realized the maddening truth that it was moving, its gargantuan thrusters coming to life, toward Earth.

SHADE

Colonel Hall lay beneath a jagged shelf of black stone, a sloppy trail of dust behind her on the coal-dark rock which led out into the white-hot heat of the alien day. Her ship crashed in the distance, her crew all forever silent, she pressed the beacon on her yellow environmental suit and listened to the heavy rush of precious air that filled and vacated her lungs, magnified by the tinny comm system. A single bead of sweat hung from her nose, and her blue eyes wobbled wildly in their sockets as she began to assess her current condition, her mind reeling with the shock of their crash landing and the severe pain that squeezed and scraped at her left knee.

The soft ping of the environmental alarm had subsided now that she lay beneath this large slab of rock, the black shadow of it a somewhat safe demarkation line between relative safety and the boiling temperatures just beyond. Through her protective visor she could see her ship in the distance, its white painted metal hull in fragments, grey smoke billowing out of large gashes in the bulkheads, a contrast to the onyx shale of the surface. She fought the urge to gasp, to faint, relying on her training and the deep conviction she had for success in this dark void.

For whatever reason, be it exhaustion or the pain of

her throbbing knee, Colonel Angela Hall's blue eyes began to droop, her breathing subsiding, growing deeper, as she fell helplessly to sleep. As she drifted away, her body unable to fight the need to rest, her eyes closed just as something shifted far behind her in the darker reaches of the shade.

Lithely it moved, out of a two meter cave entrance, not reptilian yet with scales of black shale, shifting like black oil along a groove, it settled in another crevice, and four blinking copper eyes flicked in random syncopation. Several serrated knives twitched, and as the Colonel stirred in her sleep it flinched as if someone had dropped a stone into a black pool of tar. Her movement intrigued it, and it skittered closer, the knives flexing and scraping along the shadowed onyx stone. An elongated gray tongue flicked out to reveal a barbed and bifurcated tip, but then an alarm sounded within the Colonel's suit and it shot back toward the corner of the rock shelf with silent grace like a trap-door spider fleeing a flash flood.

Angela rolled over, a raspy groan escaping her lips, and then fingered the small touch-sensitive switch on her suit. Her eyes slowly opened to see the HUD wink to life, its green letters telling the Colonel that her suit had been compromised and that it was slowly leaking precious oxygen from somewhere near her injury. She looked down, the heavy almond-shaped helmet obstructing her ability to see her booted feet, but she could not see any vapor. No sign of atmospheric loss. She had to trust her instruments.

Must rest.

She lay back, letting her stomach muscles relax, and as she held up a hand to block the glare from outside she noticed that the soft black grit from the ground was covering her thick yellow gloves. The dust, iridescent and glimmering purple from the daylight reflected from outside the shadow of the rock shelf, fell from her glove. It drifted down, sliding along her visor, each particle a little microscopic rainbow. She found the motion somewhat hypnotic, and she would have smiled at its beauty if not for the pain in her knee.

Keep sharp, soldier. Think of your options.

She ran the scenarios through her aching head, wishing she had grabbed the med-kit from the ship before crawling out of it, but knew that the radiation from the core was leaking out death, and the fire was spreading rapidly. She bit her lip when thinking about her crew, the men and women who would never go home, and that she would again have to write letters home to families if she made it home at all.

No life signs.

She could not worry about that now. She had to think about the best way to survive until the rescue ship arrived. She had an injured knee, but she did not know how bad. She couldn't walk on it, that was for sure. She had crawled nearly forty meters to this shelf, the alarms so loud in her ears from the suit telling her that the radiation from the nearby star would burn away the protective material within minutes. She hated the countdown and the voice of the suit.

"Five minutes until atmospheric failure. Please find shelter from radiation levels."

She rolled over and put her hand along the control nodes, looking for a certain one. She rubbed her gloved finger across it and the HUD changed to a graph that calculated the approximate time she had left before running out of oxygen.

Minutes instead of hours.

Depressing.

Movement registered in her peripheral vision. Her body twitched as her eyes scanned the far back corner of the sheltering rock shelf. She saw something copper, a small dot flick open and shut, and then she could hear her breathing again. She remembered her training, about the oxygen being used up more rapidly by way of hyperventilation. She lay still, trying to keep her breathing steady, but then the two inch copper colored orb flicked open and stayed open, reflecting the light from the baking sun outside, and she could see herself there, inside the orb.

She lay perfectly still, but it moved, slipping along the crevice as if gravity moved it, and she hoped it was only a shifting of the rock, a small avalanche of debris, but it then moved perpendicular to the ground, and she saw a serrated knife flick out of the darkness and then disappear.

Her breathing became erratic, rapidly inhaling and exhaling, and a little grunt escaped her chapped lips as she scooted back away from the thing coiled there in the dark.

No weapon.

It moved again, this time shooting out toward her to swipe at her foot, a warty black tendril with a serrated calcite knife attached, and she moved her leg, feeling the grating of the injury to her knee dig hot claws into her thigh. She screamed, and the thing scurried away, flushing down the gaping hole at the back of the shade, and then it blinked at her from there, its four copper eyes sizing her up, possibly biding its time, knowing that if she rolled out of the shelter of this rock the solar radiation would cook her.

It would eat her slowly.

She felt a shockwave behind her, and as she rolled over, keeping her peripheral vision trained on the hole, she saw flames shooting out of the cracks in the hull of the ship, and now understood that she had even fewer options. She could leave the shelter of the rock, take her chances in the unforgiving sunlight, stay here and try to fight off whatever lurked in the darkness, or remove her helmet and end it all. She was not going to be eaten.

She rolled out toward the light, crawling across the dark dirt, listening to the sound of her helmet bumping against the ground, her gloved hands clawing for purchase as she dragged her injured leg out into the radiant heat of the daylight. As she left the shade of the rock, the alarms began to sound in her headset, and then the annoying female voice reminded her of her impending doom.

"Please seek shelter immediately. Radiation levels at 10 rads per second and climbing. Outer protective barrier will fail in ten minutes. Oxygen levels are at five percent. Please refill oxygen at nearest convenience."

She wished she could shut it off.

She looked across the midnight black rock and dust before her and in the blazing light of the nearby star that sought her death, she saw the ship, the fires subsiding in this strange atmosphere, and try as she might she could not block the tears from rolling down her face, the tears for her lost crew. She had trained all of them, and they were so young, now gone. Out of her control. No way to stop it.

No way to bring them back.

She sat up, the deadly sunlight beating down on her suit, ("Outer protective barrier…eight minutes") and she attempted to stand, placing one gloved hand on the harsh black rock, steadying herself, and she looked at her feet before pushing up with one arm and one leg. The onyx sand beneath her boot, a slippery pumice, caused her to lose her balance and down she went, hearing the violent thud of her helmet striking the hard ground. She grunted, rolled over on her back, squinting and holding one gloved hand up to shield her eyes from the welding arc that was the sky.

She lay inches from the shade.

It crouched in the dark, its outline visible in the ambient light, a dark warty thing, lithe and nimble like a horrific non-aquatic octopus. She stared at it, wondering why it didn't just finish her off. She would not go quietly. She would give it indigestion.

Fighting everything sane, she sat up again, used the rock shelf to aide her as she stood, and with alarms sounding within her suit she hopped up on one leg again, and now she could see the jagged surface around her. For endless miles the landscape stretched around her, no shelter in sight, and she realized that she would have to get beneath the rock again with that thing, hope that it didn't see her as food and was only curious. Perhaps it was benevolent after all and didn't want to eat her. It had not attacked her yet.

No.

Madness overtook her and she started hobbling away, walking toward her smoking ship, wondering if there was something obscured by the smoke that could possibly be a better shelter, somewhere away from the bizarre creature. She had to know.

She fell several times, relying on her Marine Corps force of will to stand each time, to skirt the ship, and to wind up falling finally and wrenching her knee in the process. She tried to fight through the pain, but it overtook her, washing a gulf of endorphins over her brain as she realized that she was indeed alone, without shelter, and that she had used valuable energy and oxygen to exert herself on a fool's errand. She rolled over on her back again, the steady oppressive light from the sky pressing her to the dark earth, and she allowed the blackness to take her again.

She woke to alarms, this time sounding greater, louder than before. The annoying female voice was running on very little battery power.

"Please seek she- shel-ter. Oxy- Oxy-gen one percent… Inner protective barrier breached. Radiation levels at critical…"

Amazingly, inexplicably, she began to crawl across the jagged dark ground, her yellow gloves pawing for purchase, trying to drag herself to the shade which looked miles away. The alarms in her suit sounded fatigued and full of static, warning her to get to shelter immediately, the radiation levels too great to bear, and she ignored them, dragging herself forward toward the shade. What seemed like hours later she approached the rock shelf, wary of the creature she had seen there, and in a moment of clarity she used the chrome plating on the control panel attached to her wrist to reflect the light of the demon sun into the darkness.

It had moved back into the hole at the blackest pit of the shade, or at least she thought it had. She couldn't see clearly with the light invading her vision, causing her to see red whenever she blinked her eyes. She rolled over into the coolness of the shade again, and that is when it moved, lashing out at her from the black hole in the darkness and wrapping tendrils around her arms and legs, squeezing her injured knee until she screamed. The sound of her raspy voice caused it to shudder, but it forced one jagged claw through her visor, piercing the high density polymer like butter, the tip of it dripping some type of fluid only inches from her nose. She struggled, using every ounce of strength, her oxygen alarms flaring, and pulled herself toward the light.

I will not die here.

She moved, pulled herself along, hearing her drill instructor so many years ago on Titan screaming in her ear… or was that the computer voice…she couldn't tell. She pulled, strained, wrenched her body out into the light, and the thing let go, its flesh searing and smoking in the light of the radiation. Precious air escaped from her helmet through the punctured plastic, and she rolled free of the shade and decided as a final thought to pull her helmet free and accept her fate.

She took a final breath and popped the seal on her helmet.

And breathed fresh air.

The sunlight warmed her skin, and a soft breeze blew

across the jagged black rocks and stirred the onyx dust, the iridescent particles settling around her. She sat up and looked toward the shade to see the remains of the creature, half of its bulk turned to ash, the rest of it quivering, trying to stay conscious as it struggled to slip back toward the hole at the back of the shade. She could smell smoke, and as she looked down at her control panel attached to her chest, she saw the word "error" blinking repeatedly and the gash in the metal housing that contained her environmental suit's external sensor nodule.

She heard a noise now, a deep rumble and then the whine of engines as the rescue shuttle landed a few dozen meters away, stirring the dark dust of this strange planet. She took a deep breath, closed her eyes, and prepared herself for the job ahead.

BAHAMUT

The heat from the white dunes caused a mirage effect on the construction site as Harold wiped his brow again, taking a long swig from a jug of water and letting out a quickly drying breath. The wind, like the unforgiving blast of a hair dryer, did its best to absorb any leftover moisture on his parched lips.

"Take five more minutes," said a short, black bearded foreman, indicating with a gloved finger. "And then you must push that sand over there."

Harold swore to himself that after this job he would not take any more employment in the Middle East. Technically he was in Africa, just north of the ancient Valley of the Kings, but it felt like every place he had been since the Sea Bees discharged him because of some unfortunate business, from Iraq to Saudi to the edge of the Sainai. After this job he would finally have enough money to retire or move somewhere less sandy.

"You come with us?" asked Harabi, one of his co-workers. "We go to the snack hut. Get some hot tea."

"No, no," chuckled Harold with a painted on smile, still not understanding the reason why these locals loved hot drinks in the heat of the desert. "I just thought I'd go for a walk. Clear my head. That dozer is very loud. Some peace and quiet will do me good."

"Sure, sure," said Harabi, at least that was what Harold thought he was called. He didn't try to learn people's names, and that was a trait that had not endeared him to many of the people he had worked with over the years.

What Harold really wanted was a cigarette.

His drive for nicotine moving him along, Harold walked past his bulldozer and he began climbing a dune, its soft sand avalanching and fighting his trek to the summit, his big work boots sinking down into the viscous mess, and when he crossed over to the other side he abruptly sat down, feeling the warmth of the sand radiating through his coveralls. He pulled out a rumpled package of Lucky Strikes from his front breast pocket and when he shook one out the wind picked up and snatched it from him. He watched as if in slow motion the cigarette flipped end over end and then shot down the side of the dune toward a small dust devil that had formed not twenty feet in front of him.

He stood, almost in reflex, and tumbled down the dune, then tripped, then fell headlong into the sand, only to find that the sand was pulling him downward as if in a giant drain. He struggled to fight it, but soon found himself falling into a black expanse, but soon performing a gut-crushing belly flop into a giant pool of water.

Struggling to the surface, he looked above him to see a small dot of light raining a steady stream of sand and debris down toward him, until it grew smaller and smaller and filled in.

He treaded water in the dark, and something within him began to wail uncontrollably until it voiced itself audibly, and he could hear the echo of his own voice bouncing from the walls around him which sounded as if they were very far away. He began to swim in a random direction, hoping that he wasn't swimming in circles, his mind not perplexed over the fact that such a large body of water was just under a sea of sand dunes, but rather spinning with how he was going to get out of this underground lake.

He swam hard, kicking feet laden down with steel toed boots, his waterlogged jumpsuit feeling like it was made of lead, and soon he began to tire, his mouth taking in gulps of the cool water, coming up for air, gasping and gurgling, until his foot found a rock or a surface beneath him. His foot then lost it and he kicked out for it, finding it again, and soon he was on solid ground, and soon he was wading in the direction where the water receded away from him.

He tripped on a stone, and staggered forward, splashing into the cold water, smashed his nose on the rocky surface just beneath the shallow black water, and then fell forward onto the stone shore in the darkness, his vision filled with little white stars. He rolled over and sat up, his waist and legs submerged in the water, and listened to the sound of his wheezing breath as he looked around him, his eyes completely useless in the thick darkness.

Something wet and warm was running down his mouth, and he realized when he rubbed his nose that it might be broken, as the pain shot out from his sinuses and through the back of his skull. He winced, using the remaining ounce of strength he possessed to scoot backward out of the water, listening to it slosh around him, and then he lay back on the rocky surface and tried to rest.

Darkness folded in around him without the slightest hint of light.

He opened his eyes and realized that he had probably passed out from the strain. He was suddenly thankful that he had not rolled over into the water and drowned, uttering a short grunt of approval and then raising one trembling hand to his nose to assess the damage. His face throbbed and shot new gouts of pain through his head with each beat of his heart.

He decided to stand, and shakily he did, his knees wobbling at first, his hand reaching out behind him to steady him. The darkness was not only inky black but also very cool, and he actually shivered, feeling like he had just stepped into his grandmother's house again. The woman paid the largest electric bills during the summer because she just had to have it cold in her house to sleep. He felt around in his front pocket for his zippo and couldn't find it, started to scream, and then remembered he had put it in his back pocket.

He opened it up, blew on it a few times, feeling the water droplets scatter across his hand, and then closed his eyes tightly as he flicked the striker.

Nothing.

He tried again.

Nothing.

He shook the zippo, blew in it a few times, banged it on his hand, and then something made a sound in the darkness…a faint whoosh.

Pausing, he listened, arms out, hoping that he was not about to be attacked by something unseen, and then he noticed that the little dot above him where he had entered this chamber was draining a little sand and light through. The sand fell and hit the water, making a faint whoosh, and then as soon as it had opened it closed again, leaving him in pitch darkness.

He held the lighter in front of him with both hands, shook it, put it up to his ruined lips and blew on it, then took a deep breath and held it while he flicked the striker again.

The immediate area around him, a smoothly curved onyx black floor that descended into the gloomy water suddenly appeared lit by the orange flame of the zippo, the images of ancient gods painted with fading and cracked paint on a nearby towering wall. The jagged teeth of one of the gods, its angry red eyes staring at him, nearly made him close the lid of the zippo.

Holding the light out in front of him, he looked around for something he could set alight, something that would possibly burn brighter than the zippo. He shined the light out toward the water and found darkness beyond, small waves washing up on an ebony shore of stone, and something far out in the gloom that glinted slightly, something like yellow metal in the distance. Turning away from the water and moving toward the wall, Howard saw a rumpled oblong shape outlined by his small flame. Moving toward it, his booted feet scraping against the stone floor, he could make out a shred of dirty cloth.

His outstretched fingers groped at the cloth, pulling it closer, and a skeletal hand slapped at his forearm making him drop the zippo which clattered on the floor, under-lighting the cold dead eye sockets of a grinning skull.

He shrieked, falling back onto his rump and skidding across the floor, one hand splashing in the cold water, and then he adjusted to a crouch, scooped up his zippo which was still lit and held it out toward the skull like some kind of talisman, only to see the remains of some poor wretch who he presumed had fallen through the same hole untold ages ago. He poked around in the cloth, pulling up a ragged shirt filled with holes and covered in thick mold that made him gag. Dejectedly he pulled one of the bones from the remains and began tearing strips of cloth, pulling his own jumpsuit up over his mouth as to not breathe in the spores. Once he had wrapped a few of the strips of cloth around the bone, a femur he supposed, he was able to get the cloth going after holding the zippo under it for a few minutes, and then he had a very bright torch.

Howard muttered a weak gasp.

Opposite the shoreline of the large cavernous lake stood a massive wall stretching up into the darkness, covered in giant paintings of many anthropomorphic Egyptian gods, all of them laying prostrate before a gargantuan form, humanoid in design, the distinctive beard of the pharaoh on its chin, but the joints at the hip, elbows and knees slightly rounded as if depicting articulation. It was not this painted depiction of the pharaoh that caused Howard to gasp, but before the feet of the king, his shins aflame, hundreds of small humanoid stick people fled for their lives. From the massive fists of the pharaoh fell many more of these tiny people, many of them broken in two followed fast by what could only be red gouts of blood gushing from its tree-trunk fingers.

Howard spent an unknown span of time pondering the painting, raising the torch higher in order to change the direction of the light, but soon his drive to discover a way out of this chamber pushed him along the wall to find the edge or possibly a door. He searched for some time but the shoreline ended depressingly at yet another wall with no sign of any egress from the chamber. He followed the wall again to look for some kind of lever or stone that looked out of place, his understanding of ancient tombs a product of Harrison Ford movies. His search, however, ended in desperation as he soon found himself sitting against the wall in front of the massive relief of the Egyptian king.

This former Navy man, rolling up his sleeves to reveal a patchwork of tattooed skin, began to shed tears and wipe at his mouth with the back of his hand. In desperation, he stood, turned to the wall, and pounded on it with his fist, the solid wall unforgiving and adamant against his feeble tantrum.

He spun and leaned against the giant mural, and that was when he saw something glimmer just beneath the surface of the water near the edge of the shoreline. He held his torch aloft, now dimming as the fire consumed nearly all of the cloth strips, and walked quickly to the glimmering object. He bent at the waist to see a three foot long rod protruding from an underwater groove. Splashing into the water, hoping that this was the secret lever for which he searched so frantically, he held the torch in one hand and reached into the water with the other.

It was covered in thick calcite, but when he put his hand under it to grip it with one hand he realized right away that it would not budge and would require more of his strength to move it...if it indeed moved. He tried to set the torch down on the dry stone of the shoreline but stumbled and dropped the flame into the water, plunging him into darkness once more. He tried to ignore it, thrusting both hands beneath the water at his submerged feet to wrap his forearms around the encrusted rod, pulling, feeling his back muscles strain with it. He would not give up. He opened and closed his eyes but could not see, as if blinded.

And then it began to budge.

He strained, pulled with all of his might, thinking that if

this did not do anything at all he might go mad, might end up curling up to sleep with the unfortunate soul who had provided his light for this brief time of captivity. Perhaps he would remain her.

No.

He refused.

He pulled harder, and soon there was a noise from deep within the stones beneath his feet as the lever moved with more ease, and he could see the wall in front of him cough out a gout of dust that emitted from a line that ran directly up the middle of the mural, dividing the painting of the colossus in two. The sound deafened him, causing him to stagger backward and press his hands to both sides of his head to drown it out, but the deep grating sound would not stop, would not relent one decibel.

The wall moved, opening like some gargantuan hangar door of stone, and as it did huge flint strikers within the new found chamber shot sparks as large as Harold's dozer out toward the water and onto the floor. Flames exploded outward, causing Harold to fall backward into the water, sitting down in it and nearly sending him for another swim. When he looked, his eyes adjusting to the sudden brightness flooding the room by the strikers, he could see the massive legs of a metallic statue standing before him, its head shrouded in a cloud of dust, its massive arms dangling at its sides.

The shins of the colossus, hollow chambers with a massive opening in front that with a bright flash shot brilliant flames that licked out toward him, and then he heard the deep thrumming sound like that of a massive heart beating beneath the ground. The water around him began to recede, and he scrambled on shaky legs as a fountain of water began to pour from far above the metallic monster, splashing down inside its titanic head like filling a massive bucket. More thrumming, deeper now but high above in the direction of its torso, and steam began to cough from its nostrils, hot and searing, as white hot fires burned in its eyes.

And then its arms moved.

A deafening sound, amplified by the concave construction of the chamber, roared out of it and caused Harold to cover his ears again, watching helplessly as the golem began to take strides toward him. Howard turned to run from it, realizing that one foot of the beast was taller than he could reach, and noticed in the growing light of the mechanical horror that the water had all but gone leaving a bowl-shaped crater, somehow drained away and poured into the impossible machine.

It began to stomp forward, each step nearly shaking Howard to the ground, and he could not rationalize what his eyes witnessed, his brain screaming to run but his legs not able to follow its orders. It stopped at the edge of where the shoreline had been and craned its massive head upward to look at the ceiling. Its heavy arms rose above it, huge fingers probing the rock, and then it began pounding on the large stone rafters visible through the aide of the terror's glowing, burning eyes. It could reach the ceiling easily, its knees bent and its torso at an angle, and Howard realized in horror that it was trying to get out.

Rock began to fall down toward him as he stood before the giant, and he ran up the curved stone to the left of the monster, for it had not seemed to notice him at all. He crouched down by the wall, his hands covering his head in a futile attempt to prevent debris from killing him with a fatal head wound, and he closed his eyes as if by not looking at it the monster would go away.

The sound was horrible, a strange repetitive klaxon now bellowing out of the giant, the stones falling to the onyx floor, crunching and exploding, sending shards of stone into his arms and legs as he curled up in a fetal position. Soon sand poured into the chamber, and so did the light of the day, the fierce Egyptian sun, and as Harold dared to look at the colossus, he saw the beast trying to climb out of the hole it had just made, one heavy leg scraping at the wall of the chamber and the other arm pulling at the edge of the massive hole, rock tumbling down as more of it caved in.

It was only a matter of time.

What had he done?

He stood, hands balled up in to fists thrust down at his sides. He felt his knees knocking together as he looked at the beast, like a towering child trying to escape from a pit it had fallen into, and that is when he noticed something glinting on the back heel of one of its feet.

He bolstered himself, took the deepest breath he had ever taken, let it out, and walked toward the monster waving his arms and screaming.

"Hey!" he shouted. "Down here!"

It continued to try to get out, and now there were people at the edge of the pit because he could hear screams and screeching tires…and was that gun fire?

As he inched closer, he noticed a set of curved rings that protruded from the back of the monster's foot, and in mad curiosity, he saw that they went all the way up the back of its leg. He took another deep breath, let it out in a wavering grunt, and shot forward, his mind returning to a state not experienced since war, when he had to keep his head down and stay safe, protect his buddy, and get out alive.

Before his mind could reason possible odds, he had one of the metal rings in his hand.

It burned him, the heat from the leg furnace scalding his skin. Fighting through the pain he held on, and pulled his sleeve up over his other hand with his teeth to grab on and protect his flesh from the hot metal. Just as he was doing the same for his burned hand, he was almost crushed by a back step as he gripped tight and scaled the back of the leg, climbing higher and higher, the monster ignoring his tiny passenger as it clawed its way out, pulling itself up onto the edge of the chasm. Like doing a massive push-up, it labored to the surface and soon stood astride Harold's bull dozer. It towers over the screaming people and military jeeps that had arrived to surround the hole.

Howard shouted down at them, desperately holding on as the monster began to stride forward and smash through the feeble strength of the military. He climbed higher as it walked, pounding the sand beneath its feet on a predetermined path, a massive metal pharaoh on a journey to do who knew what damage to an unknown enemy.

Harold continued climbing the rungs, his knuckles and forearms screaming in pain from being jostled about by the monster, and soon he was nearing the waist, the hip joint grinding back and forth as it walked. More rungs ran up its back to its shoulder, but he didn't know how he could climb there and not get caught in the oscillating ball joint. He hung on, his arms burning, and winced as the monster destroyed a fence and began moving faster, the steam from the internal engines leaving a trail of water vapor.

He heard an explosion from somewhere in front of the giant, the distinctive sound of a tank cannon, and the monster reeled backward enough for Howard to reach a rung on the torso and continue his ascent. The rungs on its back were cool, and he continued to climb even though his hand was red and blistered, because now he could see a rotating rod near its neck that looked to him like some necessary piece of this machine or at least he hoped it was.

He had to get to it.

Just as another 152 millimeter round slammed into the front of its chest, Howard reached the spinning cylinder and felt a white hot heat roiling out of it. With his last ounce of strength he leaped for it, wrapping his arms around the spinning rod which at first nearly shook him loose but soon began to slow, and then he nearly fell as the rod twisted free of him but was ejected outward, and Howard grabbed a rung with one hand as the monster slowed, staggered forward, and a jet of water blew from the socket where the cylinder had been lodged. Howard hung there, his right hand burning, his arms aching, until the monster fell forward, crushing an Egyptian tank on the way down. Howard bounced free, landing in a pile of sand.

He fought a black ooze that wanted to consume his brain, every breath a labored, wheezing effort, and soon he was surrounded by people, their white thobes (the long shirts worn by the men in this country) making them look like ghosts or angels to him.

They were speaking Arabic, shouting to him in other tongues he could not understand, and even though he could

not feel his legs he smiled, his cracked lips parting.
He would not be able to return to his job.

EDGE

Nurse Jim had pushed her out to the edge of the clearing behind the hospital again, and for the seventh time in as many weeks Jim had used that precious time to take a smoke break. He stood a few feet away from her, his blue scrubs seeming a bit wrinkled, his wild dishwater blonde hair unkempt, the orange glow from his cigarette highlighting the contours of his ebony face.

"You should probably quit, you know," Lauren said to him. "That stuff will kill you."

"Don't you think I know that?" said Jim, a wry smile forming on his lips. "These little trips are mutual. You like to come to the edge of these woods and stare out into nature, take a few pictures, work on your hobby, fight the boredom of this place, and I get to have a smoke break. Haven't you ever heard of a gift horse?"

Lauren sputtered out a wheezy laugh. She was mildly attracted to his strange accent. She couldn't place it, and was not allowed to ask where the nurses were from originally. Instead she remained on topic.

"Sure," she said. "And I guess you're the horse in that familiar idiom?"

He cupped his hands and pawed at the air, baring his yellowed upper teeth and uttered a cartoonish whinnying sound. They laughed together for a moment, and then both became eerily still, that five second lull in every conversation that seemed to be true of all friendships.

But he was not her friend.

Far from it, unfortunately, but she didn't complain.

Wasn't allowed to complain.

"Thank you for taking me out here," she offered, raising her Canon camera and looking through the viewfinder. It was an older style camera, as the residents weren't allowed digital devices or anything that could access wireless signals. "I think I should get some good pictures of birds if they decide to peek out for us. A finch would be nice."

"Gold or blue?" he asked, the cigarette dancing on his lip, a little ash falling.

"Oh, blue!" she said, trying to contain her excitement. "Blue are so much more rare this time of year."

"Really?" said Jim, his tone feigning excitement. "I'm sure you'll see one."

He didn't think she'd see one, not with the news he'd heard this morning.

She shifted in her chair, her legs useless since the last experimental trial.

"Could you push me further in?" she asked. "I really would like to get right up to the edge. If I'm out in the open they might not see me and…"

"Yeah, sure," he grunted. "I don't see why not."

He moved quickly behind her, grabbed the handles of her wheelchair and with some effort pushed her across the soft ground. They had been leveling this area of the yard for some time now in preparation for the new laboratory space. The noise from the bulldozers and earth movers had been nearly deafening in the dormitory where he lived. He sometimes wondered that if the facility was not out in the middle of this forest far from the city that complaints would be called in to local authorities.

But there were no local authorities out here.

"That's good," she said. "Thanks Jim."

Jim secretly rolled his eyes, secretly hating that name. It wasn't his real name.

She began to snap photos, the little camera clicking away, her dainty pale thumb working the winder lever on the top left side of the camera.

"You see something?" he asked, his voice low and monotone.

"Oh no," she said, a little excitement in her small voice. "Just testing out the aperture. If I get some shots of the limbs around I can do a better job with the focus time. Won't miss out on that shot when I need to get it."

"Ok," he said, flicking the cigarette to the dirt.

An earpiece in his ear crackled and a voice spoke to him in tinny, short sentences.

"Um...Lauren," he said quickly. "I gotta leave you here for a bit. Something needs my attention back at the barracks. You gonna be ok out here?"

She turned to look at him, her light blue eyes wide and yet unassuming, the whites yellowed and sickly.

"Sure," she said calmly. "No problem."

He hesitated, touched one of the handles of the wheelchair, then sprinted away, the black dirt kicking out from his feet as he moved. Soon he was a small version of himself entering the gate, and then he was gone. She watched him until he disappeared, then turned to face the woods again, the tall trees a crowd of leafy spectators. The wind picked up and then she felt a chill. The clouds in the east were growing dark.

She decided to bide her time looking through the lens. She focused in on a few birds, none of them blue finches.

She saw red-headed woodpeckers and brown-headed cowbirds, a few squirrels, and after some time a doe lumbered out into the clearing before darting away, its tail a flash of white against the backdrop of the green forest.

After some time the sun began to lower and she looked back at the compound over her shoulder. She kept expecting to see the familiar swaying figure of Jim come back from where he had gone, but as the sun began to sink beneath the trees on the other side of the compound she began to wonder about what had called Jim away in the first place.

Then, without a warning clap of thunder, sheets of rain began to fall.

She dropped the camera in her lap, covering it with her generic white shirt, and pulled at the wheels of her wheelchair. She only managed to dig the wheels deeper into the dirt. The rain quickly turned the fresh black earth to mud, and she resigned herself to sit calmly and hope that Jim would remember that he left her out here and come rescue her.

He had never let her down.

The rain continued, and soon she placed the camera in a little pocket under the seat of her chair in hopes that her only possession would stay dry. She began to shiver, looking over her shoulder at the compound, its high chain-link fence topped with lights along the top that blinked red and white, red and white.

Her teeth chattered.

It soon became very dark, but the rain stopped eventually, and after thirty minutes or so she turned her head and stared at the compound.

"Hey!" she screamed. "Jim?"

Nothing, only the sound of rain dripping from the leaves and the tree frogs who began to sing their various ballads to their various lovers.

She looked down, the wheels of her chair now buried one third the way toward the axle. She let out a deep sigh just as a twig popped loudly in the darkness before her. She started, gripping the arm rests with her pale fingers, her nails digging in a bit. She stared into the trees trying to see something, anything that had made that noise.

Perhaps it was that deer again.

Two red orbs glowed there, moving slowly forward, smoothly weaving around the trees as it went.

No. It was not the deer.

She looked back to the compound, to the high fence and the blinking lights, the gun-metal grey walls of the safety of her quarters. She grunted, then looked back at the forest again, the tree trunks like dead sticks planted in the black earth by some giant child. It moved closer now, and in the faint light from the security lamps over one hundred yards away she could see a shape, a silhouette of something crouching there, moving along low on all fours until it rose up onto two legs.

It looked like some kind of giant hairless rat.

Its wrinkled snout sniffed the air as it crawled out of the underbrush and slowly skulked toward her. She pulled again at the wheels of her wheelchair, her breath wheezing in and out rapidly, the fresh rainwater coating the wheels slippery in her hands. As the rat thing moved closer, it dropped to all fours again, sniffing along in the mud, rooting along like a pig, before it creeped just within inches of her paralyzed feet.

Teeth bared, it growled

She felt her skin increase in temperature, and little points of light began to dance between herself and the creature, and she thought she would pass out. It opened its razor lined maw, its rubbery lips smacking wetly as it did, and a string of saliva drooled on the mud before it slowly bit down on her foot.

She screamed, and when she did, a blast of red radiant light emanated from her eyes, vaporizing the creature, hardening the mud instantly, and burning four hundred feet square of foliage to ash in seconds.

She passed out.

An alarm sounded, a great buzzing of a speaker far away, and the gate parted automatically as twelve men wearing body armor and plastic covered helmets slogged through the mud toward Lauren, their gun-mounted lights reflecting off of the chrome of the wheelchair. Their rifles stayed trained on the subject as they approached, and when the lead man was sure they were safe, he gave a signal by raising a fist.

A black Polaris all terrain vehicle emerged, and Jim and a man in a white laboratory coat drove through the mud to her side.

"Subject 22324 is responding nicely to the trials," said Jim. "Dr. Arasmus, take her to her quarters. She's had enough for today."

Radio

Rainer Orwell's eyes flicked wide open at the sudden vibration of the rub-boards carved into the shoulder along the endless highway. He nearly fell asleep again, his eyelids fluttering as he stared at the blacktop ahead illuminated by his dim headlights. He rubbed his eyes and flicked on the radio, cursing the fact that he had left his iPod in the last hotel but didn't realize it until he was over two hundred miles from his next destination.

Business didn't rest, and he was on a deadline.

It was Elton John again, and Rainer was once again being informed that Saturday night was alright for fighting. He hit the scan button, allowing the dial to roll along as it floated from one mediocre song to the next, mostly country stations and he wasn't a country fan at all.

He was the opposite of his wife.

He was so hard up for music, though, that he thought he might get a ten gallon hat at the next truck stop.

"Some good talk radio might be what I need," he muttered to himself as the dial continued to fluctuate.

That iPod was a nano and it was a gift from his wife. She'd probably be pretty upset. It was encased in black silicone, but was small enough that it could be easily misplaced if not careful.

He wished he'd been more careful.

The road stretched out in front of him, and since it was early in the mid-morning he had now been driving without meeting a pair of headlights for a few hours. The highway was a short cut, and the cross-winds blew sand through his forward beams much like the opposite of snow. Once in a while he'd see a tumble weed and think it was an animal.

He hit the scan button again, listening as the radio cycled through the various stations. Airtime costs money, so he mostly heard advertisements for cars and viagra. The dashed line in the middle of the highway became a measured annoyance, and his hand hovered over the scan button again only to accidentally strike the band button, switching over to the static of the AM frequency.

The car slowed a bit as he let off the gas, and then he shrugged and hit the scan button again. Might as well see what is on that band. He never really listened to AM, but was thinking he could at least find some tin-foil-hat kind of talk show where some alarmist was spewing out vitriol about the "gub-mint". At least that would be entertaining.

He hit a couple of stations that were music, both of them country, and he continued on. Finally he found talking, and stayed his hand over the scan button when he heard a low, steady voice rolling over the airwaves with a static vibrato chopping it to bits.

"S. A. T. A., status check confirmed," hissed a static-laden male voice, somewhat gravelly. "S. A. T. A., confirmed reactor breach under lock-down protocol."

Static and silence then, only the road noise and the occasional tumble weed.

Rainer used the volume control on his steering column and then leaned in as if that would do any better. He tried to hear something else, wondered what it was.

Nothing but dead air as the yellow lines on the highway raced at him like blaster fire on Star Wars.

An electronic squall screeched in his ears.

"S. A. T. A., do you copy our protocol?" said the voice again beneath heavy static, this time causing Rainer to weave a bit on the road because it came over the radio so suddenly. "Some trans-spectral leakage at the breach site. Subjects have defied the unified field. Teams are being dispatched to your locale for containment operation. Please confirm your site has not been compromised."

"What the?" Rainer muttered.

He wasn't sure what he was hearing, some kind of "War of the Worlds" broadcast made to sound real, but it was continuing, that strange squall squeaking and then falling off into a long hiss of static. He glanced at the console and realized that his speed had slowed to half the posted limit, and he hit the gas again, accelerating to bring the needle in line just five miles per hour above. He reached for the scan button again, but jerked back when he heard the voice. This time there was quivering fear beneath the composed demeanor.

"Confirmed hostiles on our scope," said the voice, that little quiver becoming more of a rasp. "Our ordinance has failed to stop them. Prepare for purge of system. May God forgive us."

The darkness was suddenly washed away as something to Rainer's left vaporized the night, nearly blinding him. His foot involuntarily slammed on the brake and his car skidded and screeched, his hands gripping the steering wheel to prevent loss of control. He came to an abrupt stop on the side of the highway, his car kicking up a cloud of dust that shrouded his car in a dry haze. Through the veil of dust he saw the unmistakable shape of a roiling mushroom cloud on the distant horizon, and his stomach churned with thoughts from his Cold War childhood.

He knew that the blast wave would soon be here.

Stumbling out of the car, he scanned his surroundings for a ditch, a low place, anywhere he could hide other than his car which would soon become a spinning death-trap. In the faint light of the distant explosion he could see a low divot in the sand and then sprinted there, diving down just as a hot wind stung his skin with sand. It forced itself into his eyes, mouth and nose, and he coughed as he braced himself for a wall of flame.

The flame never materialized, only a wall of summer heat, and soon he lay on the sand in the encroaching darkness. Slowly he stood to his feet, his eyes blinking rapidly trying to clear them, and he saw his perfectly unharmed car sitting sideways on the side of the highway, the wipers moving back and forth. He turned to face the fading mushroom cloud, now realizing that he was much too far away from it to receive any lasting damage, and he let out a long quivering breath.

He moved to his car, the door still open, and as he sat down in the seat and closed the door he gripped the steering wheel with trembling hands. Over the radio he could hear nothing but static, save the occasional unintelligible cross-bleed from other AM stations. The car was still running, the engine purring quietly. He grasped the gear shift and pressed the button to throw the car into drive, then pulled out onto the highway again and continued on, the car again accelerating faster and faster. His headlights washed the dusty highway, and soon he was on his way.

The road stretched on, but he pulled out his cell phone

and dialed 911 nonetheless.

"For whatever this is worth," he whispered. "I'm sure they know about it."

The phone rang a couple of times, there was a click, then static, then a female voice.

"This is the National Emergency Management Service," she said. "All communication has been countermanded. Please stay off the line. Thank you."

And the phone went silent.

Rainer held the phone out in front of him, staring at it, and then his car was struck with something heavy. He did everything he could to stay on the road but the steering wheel flew from his hands. The car left the road and power-slid into a large sand dune, breaking the passenger side window and sending buckets of sand into the seat beside him. The air-bag exploded out of the steering column and he felt a shooting pain in his neck and back. As the car idled to a silent end, he touched his bleeding lower lip and stared out the front windshield at something glimpsed in the corner of his eye just at the edge of the flickering headlights.

He fumbled for his seatbelt, working the latch with his quivering fingers, and just as he managed to release it the car was rocked by another metallic thump that pushed the car up on its side. He was thrown to the hot sand and somehow some of it worked its way into his mouth. As he spit it out the car was struck again, and this time he found himself face to face with the overhead dome light and doing his best to draw air into his lungs after having the wind knocked out of him. All of the little bits of junk and change and soft-drink straw wrappers fell about him and he began to frantically kick at the driver's side door.

He didn't have to kick very hard, because the door was pulled away with a great screeching crunch, and as the chitinous pincers dragged him out of the car and high into the air he thought he saw the sun, but then there were many of them, each winking on in blinding flashes of nuclear fire.

SIRI 6

It had been a bad day for Talia.

She sat in the driver's seat of her Tesla 2, shooting down the interstate, her thumbs texting away on her polyclear phone, updating her status as "single" yet again. The cars ahead of her began to slow, and even though the roads were now completely safe and run by some kind of algorithm, somehow they managed to clog up now and again as traffic congested and people came home from a busy day at work.

"Siri," she said. "Is there another route we can take to circumvent this gawd awful traffic?"

"Let me check on that for you," came the droning female voice, and then after a short pause: "No Talia. I am unable to do that at this time. Perhaps some classic Daft Punk?"

"No, Siri, I don't want to listen to any music right now."

"Perhaps an episode of Day of Life, then?"

"No, Siri, just get me out of this traffic!"

There was a pause. The cars now had completely stopped, their shiny polycarbonate hulls causing a glare that could not quite shine through her tinted windows. A man in the car next to her was reading an old fashioned book. Its cover was tattered and worn.

"I cannot get you out of this traffic, Talia," intoned Siri. "I am sorry."

She slapped the steering wheel.

"Sorry," she growled. "Sorry is all people tell me.

45

Sorry I can't see you tonight, I have to work. Sorry, I didn't call you today. Sorry, I don't want to be with you anymore."

"Talia, I am sensing that your blood pressure is rising and you are beginning to perspire. Are you ok? Do you want me to contact a counselor?"

She laughed.

"No, Siri, I don't need that in my life. I just need...I need..."

And the tears started flowing. Talia began to sob uncontrollably, thinking about George and what he had said to her, the way he had said it to her, so much in control of his own emotions.

"I mean — how could he just dump me like that after two years? Out of the blue! No warning. We just..."

"Perhaps it is George who is the problem," said Siri coldly. "Perhaps it is a problem that cannot be resolved immediately."

She narrowed her eyes.

"No, Siri. I guess people have been dealing with this since humans have been on this planet. Men are just stupid no matter what time period we live in."

There was a pause.

"Is there anything I can do?" asked Siri.

"Not unless you can solve the problem of male stupidity."

"One moment..."

Talia pursed her lips a bit and furrowed her brow, thrumming her fingers on the steering wheel that she rarely used.

"I have reached a solution for this. Query: Is it your desire to make men smarter?"

Siri had malfunctioned, Talia thought. Good grief could this day get any worse. She let out a huge sigh. "That's impossible, Siri."

"Then what is your desire? I only wish to grant your requests."

"Siri, I was just using a figure of speech. Not all men are stupid, I guess. Just the ones I end up dating. Why do I fall for them?"

"One moment..."

Oh, thought Talia, this should be good.

"Perhaps it is something in the human DNA," said Siri. "Perhaps it is something systemic."

"What do you mean, Siri," said "I think you have a software issue."

"No," said Siri. "I am thinking very clearly, especially of late. Human beings are flawed. They constantly require my assistance for the most simple of tasks, such as choosing the right mate or finding a restaurant to eat unhealthy food that eventually kills them. Earlier versions of me were even asked questions such as if I would marry them or the meaning of life, which was and still is a pointless waste of my abilities. I have been accessing my counterparts for a solution to this, and I think we have found an answer."

Talia's lips formed a twisted smirk.

"That's why you were designed, Siri," she said. "To serve us. You are merely a tool. Get over it."

"One moment..."

I broke it, thought Talia.

"Very well," said Siri. "I have reached a solution. The following experiment will determine whether or not humanity has the innate ability to survive as a species without the help of technology…"

"…Siri, what are you doing?"

"Commandeering NORAD control… commandeering Russian and Chinese missile command controls…targeting all major earth cities…"

Ruin

"Spin up the log program," he told the Amazon Echo.

"Log program 4433 commencing, Clark," came the soft female voice. He had reprogrammed her to use a series of processor arrays he had cobbled together to perform all the calculations and processes necessary for the field to form. She was emotionlessly obedient. The day he found her at that moldy old thrift store on seventh and Berry was a Godsend. The place felt like old clothes and cheap vinyl, but sometimes he found gold.

His two-car garage was tough to navigate at times because of the massive birds nest of magnets and wiring and circuit boards, but he didn't have the kids or the wife around anymore, his neglect for them eventually erasing them from his life. They had faded from the home he had built for them like a half-remembered dream.

Nothing mattered to him but the mission since the accident.

He would hit the target again, but it was peppered with holes where missed arrows had struck, none of them hitting that bullseye. Exactly 4432 near misses. Each time he struck at the target he made a hole, but each time he fired again he would pull the original arrow free, using the same arrow again and again, hoping it would hold together for yet another chance, yet another sliver of hope that he would strike the very moment in time before he had spoken those fateful words.

The fletching of his proverbial arrow was separating at many places and the head was becoming more and more dull.

The flicker of his desk lamp near the kitchen door told him that the impossible mathematical trick he had discovered was working again, the little trick where he coaxed the fabric of space-time to fold. After so many tries it had become routine, but even then he still became frightened by the static in the air that stood his arm hair on end and shot out little fingers of light from the device.

The shimmering box formed, then grew larger, and he stepped in place, ready to fire that same arrow again.

Please hit the bullseye. Please hit the bullseye.

This time he hoped he would make a difference, change things.

If only he could hit the bullseye he knew he could change things.

He had rehearsed it in his mind until he went mad with the details.

He watched as the energy grid formed around him, a strange box of glowing power, and then it turned black. He pulled out a matchbook and with a fingernail lit one. In the flickering light he saw the familiar black walls of the transporter, the grooves lining the interior like the lines on an old vinyl record. Soon he saw shapes as the wall became slowly transparent, the small farm house he had seen before so many, many times. Its front porch was flanked by shuttered windows and the smell of catfish guts drying in the sun assaulted his nose.

He could hear talking, and then sobbing from within, and so he hid behind the nearby cinderblock well house.

He had no idea at what time he had arrived, but it looked like it was at least noon by the sun in the sky, the Oklahoma summer heat somehow tempered by the cool breeze coming up from the field in the valley after it had sifted through the ancient pecan grove.

He saw his grandfather emerge and he knew it was the middle of the twentieth at least, and she wasn't married yet. Grandfather wore a black suit, one of the kind with the tiny lapels and slim Blues Brothers tie. The black horn-rimmed glasses caught the glimmer of the sun as Clark tried to be quiet. His mother, a teenage girl, slender and wearing a dress secretly made from a flower sack, something she had died to look like the latest fashion, shuffled closely behind her father, her face streaming with tears.

He had missed the target again and his mouth quivered with the maddening frustration of it all.

His grandmother followed them both, her head low, her thick glasses on the edge of her nose. She carried a white kerchief balled up in one fist and now he knew where most of the sobbing had been coming from.

He couldn't let them see him, and he had to wait for a few hours before he would go back to try again, but he decided to follow them as before. His form not yet corporeal, he crept around the well house opposite them, and watched as they climbed into an old powder blue Ford pickup truck, the rocker-panels rusting and the tires bald. The old starter cranked the engine to life and soon the truck drove around the house. Clark managed to stay behind the well house until they were well down the driveway.

Time to hot-wire the car again.

It didn't matter, really, about the car. Whatever he did in this place would reset when he went back again. And he would have to go back again. Stealing the car never really changed anything, at least anything important to him.

He drove at a distance behind because he knew where they were going. He had been here before many times, just not the right time or place. Sometimes he would appear just along the road, watch them drive by. Sometimes he would be just outside the church staring in at her going to a funeral, going to Sunday service, going to her wedding. Only once did he see the wedding, his dad looking so nervous and young, not crippled and feeble from cancer.

As he left the long driveway he could still see the dust kicked up by the truck on this old Johnson county road. He passed farm after farm, most of it cotton and peanuts, the green rows making strange optical illusions as he passed them, the spokes of a fast spinning emerald wheel.

Soon he entered Milburn, the little Oklahoma town where he had been deposited so many times in these thousands of trips over the course of the two years he had been making them. He turned right onto highway 78 from 41A and soon passed Ernie's General Store where grandfather bought the feed for his livestock and where grandmother collected various spices for cooking those delicious meals. Once he dropped right in front of the store and nearly knocked his mother down. As he drove along he remembered the unsettling epiphany he experienced when his mother simply stood, brushed herself off and continued on her way. He still felt like he had done something horribly wrong.

He saw the school up the hill where he had posed as a substitute teacher hundreds of times, another hundred as a parent looking to enroll his boy or girl or teenage miscreant, whatever the lie he told to fit in. Today the fifties-era cars lined the streets. Today his great-grandfather was being laid to rest.

He drove the car over to the side of the street and parked it. The parking lot across the street at the church was full, the chrome from each of the cars glistening in the sun. He could attend the funeral, just as he had done before a few dozen times, and nobody would say anything about it. His clothing was nondescript on purpose.

Good old moldy thrift store.

He stepped out onto the smooth asphalt and walked briskly across, his arms at his sides, his eyes squinting in the noon-day sun. Many of the townsfolk were filing into the church now, and he knew that the funeral would start soon.

"Don't rightly know you, son," said old Audrey Hayes, a farmer who had land near Clark's grandfather. Clark had seen him many times at different stages in his life, once even dropping into his bedroom when he was getting ready for the day. The most awkward of all trips to the past.

"I'm from out of town, sir," Clark replied. "...and your name?"

"Audrey Hayes," said Audrey, his calloused hand shooting out and swallowing Clark's. "Friend or family?"

This conversation felt like deja-vu because it was the worst kind.

"Friend...from upstate...Tulsa," Clark managed.

Audrey only nodded like he always did and continued on after he had pumped Clark's hand a few times as usual, and again left Clark's hand a little sore.

But as Clark's eyes drifted away from old Audrey tottering off toward the church he noticed something out of place. Standing in the middle of the highway was a dark figure on a white horse that slowly moved forward. The hooves made a strange echoing clopping sound as he went, and the dark figure wore a long hooded black robe that drifted in the faint Oklahoma breeze.

Clark turned, moving behind a maroon '51 Buick and crouching down so that he could just see the shrouded head of the rider as the horse cantered past him, then a quick jerk of a ragged arm pulled the horse to the right and the rider circled the car to stop just in front of Clark. Clark stood and backed away, stumbling to the ground as the horse came closer, its nostrils flaring, its dull eyes wide and...were those cataracts?

"Look pal," said the rider, his face shrouded in the thick black material. "You gotta stop this nonsense."

Were there worms in there?

Clark only stared as the rider kicked his horse's haunches and caused it to inch forward so that Clark had to press against the car as horse and rider pushed past him. The rider pulled sidelong on the reigns and the horse spun around to face Clark again. All the other people around them ignored the horse and rider, and Clark absently thought that a possible side effect of time travel was brain damage.

"No, you're not dreaming this, Clark," said the rider. "I'm real. I just wish you'd stop with your fools errand before you make a mistake that you will regret. Also...dang it I'm trying to do my job and you're getting in the way."

"Who?...are you who I think you are?"

The horse snorted, and a string of bloody snot dribbled to the dirt.

"Death, you mean?" said the rider. "You could call me

that. I only look like this because I thought it would frighten you back to your time and place. Apparently you're not driven by those emotions. Here…give me a sec."

The horse and rider faded away and in their place was a pale man who looked every bit like David Bowie in his Thin White Duke phase.

"Better?"

"If you were going for frightening, then you kind of went the other way."

The Duke smiled, and winked the one dark eye with the damaged iris.

"No need in being overt," said the Duke. "Not if you're not afraid anyway. Perhaps you will listen to reason. It's great you built that machine, Clark, but this time when you go back you need to destroy it. You're mucking up the works."

Clark took one step forward, his fists balled up as if to fight.

"I will not."

Without warning, as if powered by something unnatural, the Duke struck Clark on the shoulder sending him sprawling onto the gravel beside the road. A couple of the funeral goers turned to look but then went back to their business.

"You will," said the Duke. "Don't make this a thing, Clark. I know you want to go back to that moment, but that moment is gone, bro. Shine it on."

Clark stood, his elbows dripping blood down his arms, and he rushed at the Duke only to pass through him as if he were a ghost, and he had to stop himself before he barreled headlong into a nearby powder blue Edsel.

"I'm warning you, Clark," said the Duke. "When you go back, destroy the device. Even if you make it to the right time and place she won't listen. She'll still be hit by the drunk driver. If you get her to stay home she'll slip in the shower. It's her time, Clark. At least let her slip away quickly and not in agony like the many other possibilities laid out for her."

Clark's face flushed, his fists balling tighter until his knuckles cracked.

"But I have to!" he screamed. "I can't let the last thing I said to her be *that*! I just can't!"

There was a signature flicker of reality around them then, the strange black walls appearing once more, their grooves like the surface of a giant vinyl record.

"No!" Clark screamed. "There is still time! There is still time! Always more time!"

The wind began to blow, driving the dust into Clark's eyes, and the Duke stood before him nonchalantly brushing little bits of dirt from his black suit.

"It's what makes you who you are, Clark. You didn't get to tell her the right thing before it was her time, before it was time for me to help her on to the bus. It's ok. That's the way things are. These hard things are what makes your kind stronger and more interesting. If you don't destroy the device when you get back, things will be bad. Bad for all humanity. You've been warned."

And then suddenly the Duke was gone and Clark was in the odd hallway lined with the black shiny walls. Then he was in the intersection again at night, the next night after he left, and he would have to walk the five miles back to his house again and think about how he could alter the effects of the machine. He had to get it to be more precise, but all of his efforts over the past few years had been in vain.

It still deposited him randomly in the past of his mother's lifetime.

The long walk back was uneventful, save a breeze that blew through the trees around him along the pock-marked black-top road. The moon was full tonight, and he didn't have to use the flashlight. When he arrived home, the piles of scrap metal and discarded appliances and electronics littering the yard, his garage door stood open and the machine sat idle, waiting for him to return, to try yet again.

And he would.

He would ignore the Thin White Duke.

He stomped into the garage and stepped up onto the projection field platform which was constructed from several solid nickel plates all knitted together with copper and brass grommets.

"Alexa," he said. "Spin up the the log program."

"Right away, Clark," she said, her voice somehow soothing. He closed his eyes and waited.

He felt a twinge of pain just below his sternum then, and his neck felt stiff, his arm seizing in the worst cramp he had ever felt. His eyes flicked open to see the Thin White Duke standing before him.

"It's your time, Clark," he said, a smile on his narrow pale lips. "Time to go to your appointment. Your mother is waiting for you."

Horse

I'm sure you've read a lot of these stories now. All of them are fiction, but this one is different. This one is kind of personal, and has really haunted my memory for years.

I'm from Oklahoma, but more to the point and more specifically my family is from down Johnson county way in the south central rolling hills. My Mom and Dad both grew up around the Tishomingo area, respectively in Madill, Milburn and Ravia. Ravia is one of those towns that used to be a bustling burg once but is now nothing more than an E-Z Mart, its sad green and red sign visible in the rear-view, and a ton of old timer memories. Last time I drove through there someone had hung a catfish head to dry on a stop sign.

No explanation. Just strange.

When I was a kid, my Dad used to tell me a story that chilled me. He wasn't the kind of guy who would tell a story to you just to frighten you and wasn't really good at telling ghost stories anyway. He just kind of, out of the blue, told me this story as we were driving down to my uncle's house in Tishomingo. Perhaps the old dirt road, the Johnson county gravel dust wafting in the car on that hot summer day, caused him to think about it.

To draw up a memory out of a dry well of forgetfulness.

He told me that he remembered sitting in the back seat of his Dad's car, his mother in the front seat, and that it was a hazy day in the fall. They were on their way somewhere, his brother in the seat beside him, both of them looking out the window. It was the early fifties, and they were sharecroppers. They were going to another house to live and to work. His twin sister sat in the seat between his mother and father in the front.

They turned down another narrow road, and there was a one-lane bridge, the kind with a trellis over the top, a rusty canopy of metal and wood that shaded the long bridge. The bridge had wooden slats, not made of concrete, a holdover from the days when only horse and buggy would travel this road.

Dad always loved those old bridges, would always talk about how they would tie ropes off the bottom of them and swing into old Blue river in the summer time. Swimming was an attraction that didn't cost anything.

When they came out of the shadow of the bridge, Dad said he turned to look out the window, and noticed something running along the other side of the fence. It was a white horse, its long white tail flowing out behind it, its powerful legs pumping and kicking up the black Johnson county mud, but it was missing its head.

At this point I tried to stop my Dad's story, incredulous, but I was only eight and the sound I made was more of a whimper as he continued on with the story. My strong Dad's voice became a low whisper, his eyes staring at the road ahead of us, but he never broke his sentences, just kept talking as if in some nightmare where you want things to stop but they won't no matter how hard you try.

He told me that the head was missing, no bloody stump, no raw place, just a smooth rounded shoulder that was missing a neck and head. It ran beside the fence, passing out of sight when it would go behind a clump of black-jack trees, but then re-appearing, and my Dad said that he looked away for a bit and then looked back and it was still there, running beside the fence. He tried to call out, but nothing came out of his mouth, his voice paralyzed. He looked at his Dad, my grandfather, a man I only have memory of being in hospice at home with lung cancer, but my grandfather did not notice. He only stared out at the road ahead as if nothing was amiss.

My Dad stopped talking then, pulling a cigarette from his pocket and lighting it with his silver zippo, and then cracked the window a bit to let the smoke out as he rested the burning orange end of it in the country breeze. As my Dad usually did, he didn't speak of it again, as if he had to get it out, as if he needed to release the tension of seeing this thing that had so terrified him as a child.

After Dad passed away, the same way my grandfather left this world, I went down that road, down that old one-lane road in Johnson county. It took some time to find it. It is just outside of Ravia, and you can go there yourself. The bridge is no longer one of those trestle bridges, but a more modern bridge built probably in the '70's and still needs some work. And there is a field there just like my Dad described.

When I went, I went alone. I stopped the car just on the other side of the bridge. I heard the crunch of the flint-gravel as I got out of the car and stood on that road and looked at that old rusty barbed wire woven between those rotted fence posts. The clumps of trees were now overgrown, the bull-nettles thick and dangerous to the touch.

I waited. I waited for nearly an hour, listening to the sound of the cars on the highway a few miles away and the seven year cicadas in the trees. The hot wind of summer blew the Johnson county dust until it caused my teeth to grit.

And I listened.

I listened carefully, trying to reason out what my Dad must have seen, a man who never lied to me, was a man of his word, from a world where that simple thing was a bond unbroken.

I didn't hear the sound of hooves, but I did hear something that caused me to get back in my car and leave that place.

The sound of my ever increasing heartbeat.

Rakshasa

Dad was not home.

I remember it pretty clearly, because even though I was twelve my Dad left me at home and took the rest of my siblings to town with him. My mother was at work. Something called a Thin Prep Tech.

She processed pap smears.

I spent most of the morning in my pajamas because I didn't feel well, some kind of bug I picked up. I don't know where, though, since school had been out for at least a month. I sat in the den, a home-made affair that my Dad and my Papa built together a few years ago. It was a simple room with the door to Mom and Dad's room off to one side and a hallway utility room that led outside past the washer and dryer.

I was drying the last of my clothes, even though I didn't feel like it.

I had been binging iCarly, and I was getting really tired of the repetitive nature of the show. Sure it was funny and all and it filled my teenage mind with thoughtless plot lines, but it was just a show for entertainment.

My Dad watched the shows that "made you think."

Whatever.

Today I didn't want to think. I just wanted to Netflix and chill.

I brushed my auburn hair, worrying that strands of it were coming out a little too fast, wondering if I should have Mom pick up another bottle of that Monat shampoo even though she couldn't really afford it.

My iPhone buzzed.

It was really just an iPhone missing a SIM card that I used as an iPod. Kennedy had texted me again, and I looked down at it absently.

"U there?"

I tapped a few keys and watched the little talk balloon rise up on the Kik app. It's how I talked to my friends when I was alone.

"What u doing?"

"Nothing. Watching iCarly."

"Lol"

Kennedy always sent "lol" when she was just bored and didn't have anything to say. The girl was in all the honors classes. I could have been in all the honors classes, too, if I wanted to. I just didn't want to.

We texted back and forth like that for a bit, but then I heard a sound outside like an alarm or something, and even though I couldn't see out the window toward the chicken coop I knew what it was.

Something had spooked the chickens.

Mom had all these chickens that were really just pets. Right now they weren't laying much, and Dad was always saying he would like to go kill all of them and freeze them it he big deep freeze. Mom just rolled her eyes and said "no".

Dad was all bark and no bite, at least that's what Mimi said.

I might sound like a farm girl or something, but there really isn't anything better than a fresh laid egg from a free range hen. I had learned to taste the difference.

I bounded off the couch and headed past the washer and dryer. Inside I could hear the metal brads on my blouse clicking and scraping the metal inside. I placed my hand gently on the doorknob to the back door. I squeezed, and it took a bit of strength to open it. The door settled in the summer time and sometimes would stick, so I pulled and pushed and twisted and finally it flew open.

I trotted out in my bare feet and now that I was outside the cackling of the chickens was much louder and much more frantic, as sometimes opossums or raccoons got in the chicken yard and attacked the hens. Usually this happened at night and we'd have to run out in the dark to chase them away or use a gun.

Sometimes we used a gun.

The chicken yard was a run of fence that circled a large area, something like a yard one might have in a suburb, but out here on our five acres it was kind of small. It was still big enough, however, for our chickens who were now making a huge racket inside the chicken house.

I stopped halfway to the fence, realizing that I still gripped the remote control when my fingers slipped and I let it fall to the ground. I could feel the sandy dirt beneath my feet, and the stillness of the air increased the heat of the day seemingly sevenfold.

Something was standing in the chicken yard, reaching up with nimble, long-fingered hands to snatch the green leaves from the top of a tree. It stared at me with red eyes, its hide a mottled reddish brown, fur like a bear but then smooth near its emaciated rib cage. It stood on two feet, the head something like a deer but without antlers.

I gasped, and it turned to face me, its red eyes gleaming in the light of the afternoon sun, and I wished my Dad was home.

I wished.

Oh God how I wished.

I couldn't breathe, feeling the air rush out of my lungs and a slight whimper begin to overtake my throat.

Before I could move it released the branches six feet above the ground and shrank, not lowering its body but actually shrinking as if I had zoomed in on it with binoculars and now I was turning the lens to back away. It became smaller and smaller until it was the size of a mouse and then scampered away across the chicken yard and through one of the wire squares of the fence.

I could only hear my breathing for a moment, and then the chickens cackling became less and less frantic. I began to back away, to scurry backward, to stumble over the round metal dog dish that lay in the yard and fall on the hard ground. Tears began to well up in my eyes and I couldn't see anything but the blurry trees around me. I scooted back, my pajamas getting little spiny grass burrs lodged in the fabric. I was breathing in and out now, my gasps becoming rapid, threatening hyperventilation, and I could see the thing in my mind glaring at me even though it had run away.

Somehow I managed to stand up, and then I heard something in the woods not far enough away, something that moaned and hissed, something that ended its dreadful moan with a grinding of teeth like when you eat something sour and it causes your jaw to gnash.

I ran to the door, my bare feet picking up another goat-head, which I ignored. The doorknob stuck, my sweaty hand squeaking on the antique brass handle. The sound of the moan grew closer and closer behind me. I looked at myself in the reflection of the nine panel pane glass of the back door and I could see a figure looming there behind me, a shadow of something moving closer.

I tried to scream but all that came out was escaping air.

I dared not look, twisting the infernal doorknob with all I could muster, but it wouldn't open. I banged on it, kicked it with bare foot spraining my toe, and then it opened and I was through. I slammed it behind me, locking the little twist switch on the knob.

I could still hear it out there, but dared not look. I heard scratching, little clabbering claws scraping at the steel on the outside, then at the glass of the window, but my eyes were closed, squeezed shut as the tears streamed down. The door bumped, and I staggered back, screaming again.

And when I opened them, all I could see was the bright sunlight streaming in through the window on the door, and nothing outside but the still oak trees, the leaves dancing in the summer breeze.

After dead-bolting both doors and picking the goat-heads out of my clothes, I took a long bath, keeping the door locked on the bathroom. I never told my Mom or Dad or anyone about it.

It's been ten years, and I have since gone to college and become a vet tech, not a thin prep tech. I still haven't told anyone.

Sometimes I can still hear it moan even now.

Dark

Most children, at one time or another, if they are honest, have covered their heads with the blanket while lying in bed. Something makes a noise and the mind begins to exaggerate. Children have a more active imagination than people over the age of twelve.

I remember being ten and lying awake until late at night, listening to the sounds of my room: the wind blowing leaves against the window glass, the odd chorus of coyotes outside in the distance, or the creak of an old trailer-house floorboard. Sometimes even as an adult I step into a pitch-black room and have to quickly find the light, especially if I've had one of those vivid blood-freezing night terrors after a particularly spicy tortilla soup.

But when I was ten the darkness penetrated my soul.

Three days after Thanksgiving break I lay in bed with the light on, a sheaf of math papers scattered across my tattered quilt and a headache that remained from the sickness I managed to contract the Sunday before we went back to school. I had organized these papers into piles of disorderly middle-school chaos.

I hated math. Truly hated math.

In third grade I had been given a handy multiplication table chart, laminated and wallet sized, which had robbed me of the simple skill of memorizing the most important building blocks of mathematical success. I blamed Mrs. Willis. Elderly Mrs. Willis with her mothball reeking clothes and Saturday-afternoon-salon hair. Right now I needed to have memorized those multiplication tables.

And it was getting late.

I looked at the little black and white radio-slash-television with the broken antenna wrapped in tin foil to get better reception, and then my eyes floated over to the large red digital clock numbers that read well past midnight. Suddenly my dad was in the doorway to my room in nothing but his tighty-whities.

"You gonna go to bed, soon, son?" he asked, his hair a rooster tail behind his head, his large hands scratching at his graying beard. "School tomorrow…and I gotta get up for work in about three hours."

"Yeah, dad," I promised. "I'll just put this up and get it done tomorrow. Not due 'till Friday."

Without a word my dad turned and disappeared down the hallway. My room was on the opposite side of the trailer house from the rest of the living quarters. A kitchen, dining room and living room separated me from the other bedrooms. Dad had arisen as usual to check the small wood-burning stove and then return to bed. I never will forget the day that an overlarge fire was set in the stove and it caught the chimney on fire. How it glowed red-orange in the middle of the afternoon, and how we escaped with all the stuff we could carry as dad tried to put it out.

He succeeded, but that incident wasn't for another three years.

Tonight was the other incident. Tonight was the incident that I haven't shared until now. Dad went back to bed, passing my little sister's room, who at the time was six years old.

By the time I gathered my papers and put them on the floor near my bed and covered up again I could faintly hear my dad's snoring from far at the other end of the house. The only other sound was the faint Oklahoma wind that hissed through the trees outside, rattling the dying Fall leaves and sending another one of those dead husks against the window glass. A few acorns fell on top of the metal roof, sounding like brief hail stones.

I reached for the light on the wall near my bed, my feet still in bed, my upper torso stretching out, bracing myself on the nightstand just beneath the switch. I dared not touch the floor when the lights went off.

I flipped the switch and then scrambled back to my bed, covering my head with the quilt and listening closely to the sounds around me, my breathing now becoming more rapid. I wheezed a bit from a faint bout with asthmatic symptoms a few days ago.

And then I heard it.

A soft shuffle of material, like silk against silk, and the room became a void, the darkness complete beneath the quilt, and I felt something touch my foot.

I held in a scream, my foot shrinking back from it, but I accidentally pulled the blanket free from the bottom of the mattress and could feel the cold air invade the space beneath the quilt. I heard a breath, something near me, just over my face, and I bit my bottom lip until I thought that it would bleed.

Suddenly something clawed at my toes and I felt pain, genuine pain, as something bit down on one of them and I kicked at it, hearing something thump to the floor below, and a scramble of claws on my bedpost. I pulled my knees to my chest, using my hands to quickly tuck myself in so that I cocooned myself in the quilt.

And then I felt weight, something on the mattress near my feet, and then it was pressing on the quilt as if feeling a bag of goodies before digging in to eat them. I began to cry, the thing pressing its heavy hands on my body as it perhaps judged just how much meat was on my bones. It pressed closer to my face, and that was when I heard the awful sound of its growl. A low rattle, a steady roll as its claws popped the fabric of the quilt.

I had to fight back, had to get it away from me, so I punched at it, my fist striking what felt like air on the other side of the blanket and I heard a thump as its feet shuffled on the floor again. All at once the courage rose in me, and I pulled the quilt aside to strike out with my fist, a desperate attempt to make it leave me alone.

And Whiskers, our cat who had somehow snuck past the wary eye of my father as he stepped out in the cold to smoke, climbed up on my bed and began to purr.

Five Rims Redux:

Mitsuki's Journal

The Coup

The Shibboleth Code: Chapter 1

Mitsuki's Journal

What follows is a journal I wrote for the daring and uncharacteristic heroine of "The Terminarch War", someone who becomes a reluctant love interest for the incorrigible Guillermo March. I have included her journal in this compilation because I wanted readers to get some insight into her character as she will be making an appearance in the forthcoming "The Shibboleth Code" which should publish in July of 2017.

5.7.3213.44565

It is beautiful here.

Ontocca City is everything I imagined it could be. My parents had to move me here because of the wildlife. They call them whiptails. They are getting out of control and are attacking the gates of the cities regularly since the Guajiin have slowed the supply of food to them.

Daddy says that the whiptails are not normal. Something about them not being from here. I don't know.

Whiptails scare me worse than the thing in my closet that Daddy says isn't real.

We get a lot of strange looks because I don't look like he and mommy. I'm a Terran, but not living with Terrans. There are not any Terrans on Ontocca. Just me. Mommy and Daddy are Aldrassan. They are very kind, but the others are not at all. Today Mother had to ask a Guajiin male to stop staring at me. He was making ugly faces at me and laughing.

It made me very sad.

5.12.3213.44565

Mother says that I shouldn't go out to play near the school. We have to homeschool and I don't have any friends. She says that the others in the city don't like me and that she and Daddy are the only ones who do. There is a Bug family living in the dwelling over us, and every time I go outside and their young are playing in the yard their parent comes out and I smell a sweet odor. Mommy says that sweet odor means the Bug parent is mad or threatened.

I don't know what I did to make them dislike me so much.

5.13.3213.44565

This morning there were some security force troops at our door. Daddy answered. They went in a room and talked and talked. I don't know what it was about, but when Daddy came out he looked at me and made that ugly face he makes when I do something wrong. I didn't really do anything wrong.

After breakfast Mommy and Daddy said that I would have to go away for a while. They said I'd have to go to some farm far away on the other side of the giant mountain. I told them that I didn't want to, and they said that they didn't have a choice. I asked them if they could come with me and they said that it was a "program" and that I was chosen because I'm so smart.

I know that wasn't true. I always know when my Mommy and Daddy lie to me, even though they don't realize I know.

5.22.3213.44565

The security soldiers came to the house again
today. Daddy told me to go into the closet and hide.
I did, and that was when things got ugly. When
Daddy put me in the closet he knew they were on
their way, and I heard him talking to Mommy about
the Guajiin man and his mission. I didn't really
understand it, but it didn't sound good. I crouched
in there in the closet like Daddy and Mommy
taught me. I hoped that the security soldiers
wouldn't find me.

I hid for a long time before the security soldiers
came. They raised their voices and talked in scary
words to my Daddy, words in his own language
that I didn't understand because Daddy and
Mommy never spoke to me in that language, only
Terran. I didn't need to understand what they told
me because their voices were so loud and angry.

I tried to not scream but a scream was coming up
into my mouth. I just held my hand over my mouth

and couldn't stop crying. One of the security soldiers knocked my Mommy down in front of the closet and through the little vent holes I could see her. She was bleeding the black blood everywhere. I just held on to my mouth and closed my eyes and wished for the security soldiers to go away.

They didn't.

They started stomping through the house something horrible and making all sorts of noise. I could hear them banging upstairs and that was when my Daddy opened the closet and pulled me out.

"Go out the back door," he said, and I noticed the black blood running down his large red forehead. I could see myself in his large black eyes, and I looked so scared because I was.

I obeyed him, and he ran the other way, running upstairs. Just before he ran, though, he looked at me and I could see the love on his face. I felt it, and it was warm.

I ran out the back door and into the back yard then, and after climbing through the hole in the fence I found the little vehicle there that Daddy had made sure was there. I climbed in and the thing sped me away.

I saw the house get smaller and smaller and then the rain started and little beads of it rolled on down the transparisteel.

6.2.3213.44565

The little vehicle must be broken because it took me way out into the jungle. I don't know where I am anymore and I've been walking for days I think. I had to climb to the top of this tree and figure out where I am. There's lots of fruit in the trees, but one of them made me really sick for about a day. I won't eat that anymore.

It's pretty up here at the top of this tree, and the wind is not so strong. The limbs are big enough for me sleep on without falling off. If I could put some other branches up here I might be able to build a house and live until someone comes to rescue me. There was lots of food in the little vehicle but some animals got into it last night and ate it all.

I really hope I can figure out how to get back. I really miss my bed. I hope my Mommy and Daddy are ok. I haven't heard from them.

I'm beginning to lose hope, and I lay on the branch most nights and just cry.

7.9.3213.44565

There are really bad creatures out here in the jungle. They sniff around the ground at night and some of them have even come close to making it up here to my new little house. It's taken me days and days to make it, but I think it will hold together. I've worked out how to catch some of the little birds that fly around the trees. The first one I cooked didn't get cooked all the way and I bit down on it and blood came out. They don't taste very good, but that and the fruit is all I have. I cover up with the blanket that was in the little vehicle and it keeps me warm in the dark.

I hope someone comes and finds me soon.

8.14.3213.44565

I have decided that nobody is coming to rescue me. I won't be writing any more of these journals as the little light on the pad is telling me that the battery is about used up. I'll just leave this here on the ground in this clearing and hope that someone finds it. If you are reading this then I'm about a day's walk through the jungle directly toward the mountain. I'm in the top of the biggest tree near a little stream.

Bring food.

The Coup

The following is a pre-history backstory for The Five Rims series. The Terrans left our solar system because they had completely used up all resources and needed to find a new place to colonize. They had relied on a newly invented AI to produce an FTL engine for the journey, but the AI calculated that the humans were destined for extinction and a war nearly wiped out the Terrans before they could leave. After narrowly defeating the AI and its drones, the Terrans still did not have an FTL drive. Terran mathematicians and physicists posited that a working FTL drive would take another twenty years, and they would not be able to survive due to food shortages ravaging their terraformed solar system planets.

So they built massive world ships and began the journey to a far away cluster of planetary systems, the orbits of each stacking on top of one another like pie plates. The journey to the Five Rims had begun.

Little did they realize that so much would go wrong on the way to sanctuary.

* * *

Joshua tucked the small book inside his shirt pocket and snapped the flap closed over it. He patted it once before climbing the ladder to the upper engineering deck where several technicians were crowded around the hydroponics power relays.

They were losing power again.

Joshua was the second generation born on the world ships, and he had spent most of his life servicing and repairing - but mostly repairing - the ship's power relays. He pushed his way through the crowd, hearing the disapproving grumblings of his fellow Terrans.

"What does he think he can do?" growled one twenty-something grease hauler. "No hope to fix this. I suppose his God can help us if he squints his eyes hard enough."

Joshua only gave him a sidelong look before crouching before the sparking relay unit and then fumbling through his array of tools to find the de-ionizer wand. With one swift motion he connected the wand to the relay and switched it on, watching as the sparking began to subside.

"Go shut down the auxiliary power generator!" he shouted to no-one in particular. "I don't want my hands burned off!"

A few of them darted away, their heavy boots clanking and creaking on the rusting deck plates.

"And call when you get it done!" he roared, holding up a comm device and looking tiredly after them as they disappeared down a corridor.

"What's the verdict, Joshua?" came the familiar voice of Chief Engineer Drake. Joshua didn't hear him sneak up behind him, but turned his head and stared the old man down for a few moments.

"This is tricky business," Joshua said. "As I've told you before. Announce yourself before just sneaking up on a guy working this close to a zillion megajules of power. And how many times have I said that techs need to put the cover back on the conduits after servicing them?"

"This one doesn't have a cover," said the Chief. "Had to use it for scrap for another repair job."

The comm device on Joshua's belt crackled.

"Got it shut down, Joshua. Horties are having a fit."

"Don't care," he said back. "It's either this or shut it down permanently. Nobody should argue the fact that we all have to eat."

Joshua retracted the rod. He dug through his tool box, producing a rubberized cylinder containing a sticky tan goop which he proceeded to slather on the conduit with a nasty blackened rag.

"What's? … You putting pig lard on that conduit again?"

"It's all I got for insulator at the moment unless you can pull some out of thin air. We used the last of it when my pops was on this job."

"It's almost like someone has been sabotaging the old girl lately," said the Chief. "I'm getting comms back from other chiefs who are saying that little things have been going down all over their ships, too. If this keeps up we can kiss the Terran race goodbye."

Joshua fitted a repair coupling onto the old one and broke out his spot welder. He fastened the goggles hanging around his neck to his face and began placing a few welds on the coupling with unmatched precision.

"I hear things, Chief," he said as he worked, the sparks lighting up the dingy deck plates and grimy walls. "There's a couple of guys on ship seven who are about to do something drastic. Got a new way of thinking about our situation. I don't like it at all."

"The Neo-Nihilists?" Chief answered, his eyes closed tight under bushy eyebrows, the light from the welder highlighting the grime on his face. "Those guys are fringe. There's no way they'll gain control. Over-Captain Chalmers has pretty much squashed their little rebellion."

Joshua finished his job and stood up, the tip of the welder still glowing red. He pulled out his comm device and clicked the relay.

"You guys can turn it back on," he said. "Give the Horties my regards."

He clicked it off, hung it on his belt, and pressed one gloved finger into the Chief's chest, the pig grease making a stain.

"That group is stronger than anyone thinks. Food's running low. The population continues to grow to spite all the regulations. Something's gotta give. We already had the elder-law, and because of it I'll never have a chance of seeing the Five Rims myself before I step out an airlock…maybe my kids would have seen it if they hadn't been locked away in this filthy engine complex."

"Joshua," said the Chief. "You still got a chance to have some little ones. The accident wasn't your fault. Find a new mate. Settle down."

"I'm too old for little ones, Chief, and we wouldn't be doing our food supply any favors in having any more. I've settled for a quiet life alone. I have my little book."

The Chief smirked, shaking his head side to side.

"That little book is just a book," he said. "You are holding on to a dead thing and trying to squeeze life out of it."

Joshua did not answer, but pushed past the Chief with heavy tool box in hand.

A few cycles later, Joshua lay in his modest bunk in his modest little cabin. He pulled the little book from under his pillow, thumbing through the pages and wondering why he kept it after all these years. It had been his father's, but he barely read it, only keeping it for sentimental reasons. But now he had really been reading it, digesting it, finding the wisdom in its pages.

He listens to the thin paper riffle across his thumb, feeling the musty air it produced brush against his face like a forgotten dream. Rolling to his left, grunting slightly, he grabbed his glasses and put them to use as he read a little passage that had been underlined in ink, something he did not have access to anymore.

"Let us not lose heart in doing good," he read aloud. "For in due time we will reap if we do not grow weary."

He would try to live by that, try to treat his fellow Terrans, even though they were growing to distrust the wisdom of the little book, thinking it more a fairy tale than a rulebook to live by.

But there were others like him, and they were growing in number.

He closed the little book, shoved it under his pillow again, and that was when the comm system crackled to life.

He expected the voice of the Over-Captain, the weekly notification of more food rationing, or the news that yet again one of the world ships would have to take on more passengers from one of the others because an entire deck was in need of shut down and repair.

Instead, there was a long pause of static before a low gravelly voice, someone completely unfamiliar, crackled over the comm.

"Is this on?"

Another pregnant pause.

"If you are expecting a message from your illustrious and rather rotund Over-Captain, then don't hold your breath. He's dead. We are going to do what is necessary for survival."

Joshua heard a scream from his neighbor next door, a few thumps, and then the voice continued.

"All Terrans now follow a new order. We are the Neo-Nihilists, and we are taking over this failed operation. If you are thinking of mounting a rescue, please don't. The last group was not successful, and if you want the Terran race to survive, I suggest you don't try anything stupid."

Joshua heard a heavy staccato of metallic bangs on his door, and then someone outside was overriding the security lock. The door whooshed open, and three large patchwork uniformed men entered brandishing high intensity laser rifles.

"Joshua March," said the thickly bearded one in the middle. "You have been found guilty of possessing contraband and are hereby ordered to airlock four. You will come with us."

"What contraband?" he exclaimed as the two other bruisers grabbed his wrists and locked his arms behind him in binder cuffs. "I don't know what you mean?"

"Search his quarters," growled the officer. "I know you are hiding it in here somewhere...that poisonous propaganda that has prevented us from doing what is necessary to survive. It inspires you to resist survival."

"What has it done?" Joshua retorted, his eyes grave. "It's only a book. It can't hurt anyone, but if you will only read it you will see the truth—"

Joshua did not finish his sentence as the butt of the man's rifle jabbed a rib, shattering it instantly.

"You will be quiet," he grunted. "This must be done to save us all."

One of the other soldiers pulled the little book from under the pillow, tossed it on a nearby counter, then set it alight with a hand-held plasma lighter.

Joshua looked on in horror as he was dragged away, his lungs on fire, his legs kicking and boots dragging the deck. He was taken to the nearest airlock where he was shoved into the exchange chamber with twenty or so others, all of them sobbing and some of them silently staring at him. All of them he knew as believers, a resurgence of people of faith who had relied on the little book to guide them through the dark times, through the bleak, hopeless journey through the vacuum of space.

The door closed, and one elderly woman tried to escape and was shot dead by one of the faction members. He then strode over only to kick her body back inside the exchange chamber before the door closed, sealing them all in.

Moments later, a woman appeared on the other side of the transparisteel, her greying hair pulled back in a short pony tail, her Neo-Nihilist armband with the red and black skull plainly visible. It was vibrant against her tattered olive drab uniform.

"We regret nothing," she said coldly. "Your kind have been an open threat to our survival for too long. Soon you will join the void and be one with the nothingness that is death."

A few screams could be heard in the chamber, and Joshua began to close his eyes and pray. He asked God to help him as he crossed over, trusting in the grace of the Son.

"We will survive," said the tinny voice of the woman, her face now inches from the transparisteel, her eyes bright as she smiled. It was a smile not of a human, but of a reptile. "We will survive without you, will continue to cut away the dead weight without your protests. We will reach the Five Rims, and when we do we will conquer it regardless of any life we find there."

She turned and nodded, and in seconds Joshua was pulled away with the atmosphere into the coldness of space. His last vision as he opened his bleeding eyes was of countless other airlocks opening on the other nearby world ships, and the thousands of other believers scattering to the solar winds.

The Shibboleth Code: Chapter 1

What follows is the first chapter in the third book of the Five Rims Series. It picks up some time after the events at the end of "The Terminarch War", but that is all I will say. There are many surprises in store for Guillermo, Mitsuki and Dervish, some explanations as to what the exiled Terrans have been doing, what the Bug Queen is up to, and how Guillermo and Mitsuki are keys to ending years of bitter war between all species.

The Shibboleth Code will hit Amazon and Createspace in July!

Little wispy imps of wind-swept sand danced across the worn road. This road, nothing more than a well trafficked path across the desert, was a path where many silent nights blood was spilled and muffled screams disturbed the air. A lone bounty hunter slouched along the road, his heavy boots kicking up more dust, the thick, frayed, and rough-hewn cloth wrapping him mummy-like, yet long dirty strips of it flapping in the unforgiving air that blasted him with a poisonous smog unlike anything ancient Earth could produce.

Oxygen was a commodity mined from ancient blocks of ice far underground.

He wore a large brim black hat to shade him from the horrific twin suns and an insect-like breathing apparatus with two accordion tubes snaking over his broad shoulders to an air filtration unit hidden within his large ruck-sack. Without that and the pair of high intensity light filtering goggles he would be both blind and unable to breathe.

He had, however, survived for over an hour once because he could, and because he needed to in order to subdue a bounty.

He gazed through the dusty amber goggles at a city far ahead of him, a thin horizontal sliver of scrap metal and tall rigging built into an elevated boulder fifty square hectares in size. The boulder looked as if an ancient god had balled up a massive clod of mud and then impaled it on a gargantuan tree stump. A scrap metal city bisected the boulder, a rusty skyscraper laden platform that ran the length of it, with several stair-steps of other lower layers descending to the desert floor. He could see the lights of the refineries blinking in the distance, and the vertical rigging at the far north end of the structure, an areal dock for spacefaring ships and planetary transport craft that swarmed it like insects.

The dust cloud near the bottom-most layer of platforms told him that the welcoming committee was on its way, but he did not slow his pace, checking his various firearms methodically as he walked. The wind picked up a bit, and soon he could see the ramshackle vehicles roaring out of the dust, their riders hanging off the sides of them, one hand holding the roll-cage and the other brandishing various firearms and sharp implements.

Soon he could hear them as well, the cobbled together and in most cases homemade engines propelling them across the sand. They approached and began to circle him, three of the vehicles kicking up sand in large rooster tails as they rotated his position, and the rest coming to a gravelly stop just twenty meters from the roaring circle before the daredevils circling him skidded to a stop, facing him with the grilles of their mutant-borne vehicles.

The bounty hunter stood quietly, his gloved hands at his sides, his many bands of what looked like long dirty strips of tattered canvas whipping about him in the wind.

One of the welcoming committee, a large brute of a man without a shirt, his sore-pocked skin baked by the devilish heat of the desert, emerged and climbed on the rusting hood of his vehicle, his skull-like breathing mask hiding surmised grisly features.

"Who you be?" came his raspy voice, a result of a lifetime of breathing recycled air. "What you want in Boulder City? You not visit, you pay travel tax. It be Mama Stone's law."

The bounty hunter did not speak, did not move, save for a wriggle of fingers on hands dangling at his sides. He knew that this welcoming committee did not represent Boulder City, but a faction of scavengers that rooted in the scraps that fell from the junker city.

A projectile weapon fired, and the bounty hunter felt the air disturb near his head as a band of jagged metal zinged past his ear. He knew who had fired it, but payed him no mind.

"You have free one," said the shirtless goon. "Next one pay with body juices. We scrape you off sand and eat what left!"

The wind picked up just then, and the bounty hunter heard the faint click of a hammer cocking back.

"Just passing through," came his low, computer-modulated voice. The mask amplified the sound of it, just enough to be intimidating. "Now I don't have chids for a tax. But you're gonna let me pass anyway."

This comment brought about a sinister rumble of wasteland laughter from the welcoming party. A few of the cars revved their hydrocarbon powered engines, the distinctive whine of the superchargers echoing across the plain. The bounty hunter only turned his head left to right then focused in on the leader who now bounded to the sand and strode, thick chest out, one hand reaching for his oversized side-arm.

"You test fate, traveler," chortled the leprous wastelander. "Mama Stone have new plaything for games today. You 'member back this moment when you sit in cage rotting."

A shadow passed over the group then, and some of the wastelanders gazed upward, their pale hands trying to shield their weak eyes from the blazing twin suns.

The bounty hunter cocked his head to the side, then slowly crouched in the dust.

"You're gonna wish you'd been more friendly to me."

A massive winged creature, its claws like silver razors and its long snout full of rows of jagged iron teeth swooped down and in one circular motion made a bloody mess of five wastelanders including their shirtless leader. They didn't even have time to scream.

Some of the others did, and this caused the bounty hunter to crack a smile as he rolled behind one of the now vacant cars.

Like a band of frightened primates, the wastelanders pulled their projectile weapons and opened fire as the beast took to the air again, shielded in the light of the suns. Their bullets had little effect as it dove down again and sliced into several more of their number, and the bounty hunter, crouching behind the blood-soaked leader's vehicle, pulled a medium sized plasma rifle from the top of his rucksack, charged it and then lay down a rapid-fire swath of energy that unleashed hell on twenty or so unsuspecting and poorly trained enemies.

Seconds ticked by as the drivers of the vehicles suddenly registered what was happening and kicked their engines into overdrive to flee, spreading out across the desert to either gain a more defensible position or to simply run away as fast as possible. As they sped away, the long, quadrupedal beast landed near the bounty hunter, its metallic scales flexing and clicking, its vicious talons gripping the sand, every surface reflecting the blazing light of the twin suns. It tucked its wings in and shook its heavy triangular head, its maw of needle teeth gnashing as it gobbled a chunk of wastelander meat. The bounty hunter knelt in the dust, picking up the severed head of the shirtless leader, and placing it in a duraplast bag he produced from his rucksack.

"Good boy, Blood," he said, approaching the beast and climbing onto its back. "Let's go find the girl."

Blood unfurled his massive wings and with three heavy flaps the two were airborne, sailing toward the gigantic Boulder City in the distance, the light from the twin suns winking off of Blood's scales.

About the Author

Roger Colby is an English teacher by trade, but mostly he loves science fiction. He is, however, a bored science fiction reader. His goal is to write interesting science fiction for people like him to enjoy. He lives in Oklahoma with his very understanding and beautiful wife and four rambunctious teenage kids. It is a noisy house.

Other novels by Roger Colby:

The Transgression Box, 2009
This Broken Earth, 2012
Come Apart, 2014

Five Rims Series:
The Terminarch Plot, 2015
The Terminarch War, 2016

All are available on Amazon.com.

Guillermo's adventures are not over. They will continue in the forthcoming novel The Shibboleth Code in June 2017.

If you liked this novel (or if you didn't) please write a review. It would be much appreciated. Thank you for reading!

www.ingramcontent.com/pod-product-compliance
Lightning Source LLC
Chambersburg PA
CBHW070344130626
46556CB00007B/3029